Nate Likes to Skate

Nate Likes to Skate

BRUCE DEGEN

I Like to Read®

Holiday House / New York

Copyright © 2016 by Bruce Degen
All Rights Reserved
HOLIDAY HOUSE is registered in the U.S. Patent and Trademark Office.
Printed and Bound in November 2015 at Tien Wah Press, Johor Bahru, Johor, Malaysia.
The artwork was created with graphite pencil and colored pencils
on Fabriano Artistico 140 lb. paper, soft press surface.
www.holidayhouse.com
First Edition
1 3 5 7 9 10 8 6 4 2

Library of Congress Cataloging-in-Publication Data
Degen, Bruce, author, illustrator.
Nate likes to skate / Bruce Degen. — First edition.
pages cm. — (I like to read)
Summary: A boy who likes to skate and a girl who likes
hats become friends, despite their differences.
ISBN 978-0-8234-3456-5 (hardcover)
[1. Stories in rhyme. 2. Friendship—Fiction.] I. Title.
PZ8.3.D364Nat 2016
[E]—dc23
2014048568

ISBN 978-0-8234-3543-2 (paperback)

For Dr. J. Malin, orthopedic surgeon:

I'd like to thank you, Dr. Joel,
A skillful, kind and thoughtful soul.
You fixed me up and made me whole;
I'd like to thank you, Dr. Joel.

Nate likes to skate.

Kate likes hats.

"Kate, do you skate?"
Nate says.
"It's great!"

Kate says, "No, Nate.
I hate to skate.
Do you like my hat?"

Nate says,
"I hate that hat.
It's a great big bat."

Kate takes it off.

Nate skates on a grate.

He falls flat.

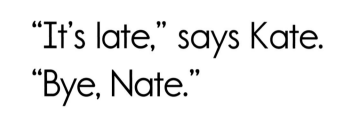

"It's late," says Kate.
"Bye, Nate."

Kate says,
"I was a brat too.
You can try my hat.
Can I try to skate?"

Nate says,
"This hat looks great."

Kate says, "Look, Nate!
I can skate. Wheeee!"

Now Nate and Kate skate . . .

and wear hats.

And it feels great.

Some More I Like to Read® Books in Paperback

Car Goes Far by Michael Garland

Come Back, Ben by Ann Hassett and John Hassett

Crow Made a Friend by Margaret Peot

Ed and Kip by Kay Chorao

Fireman Fred by Lynn Rowe Reed

Fix This Mess! by Tedd Arnold

Hiding Dinosaurs by Dan Moynihan

A Hippo in Our Yard by Liza Donnelly

A Hole in the Wall by Hans Wilhelm

I Said, "Bed!" by Bruce Degen

I Will Try by Marilyn Janovitz

Late Nate in a Race by Emily Arnold McCully

Look! by Ted Lewin

Nate Likes to Skate by Bruce Degen

Pie for Chuck by Pat Schories

Ping Wants to Play by Adam Gudeon

See Me Dig by Paul Meisel

Sick Day by David McPhail

Snow Joke by Bruce Degen

Visit http://www.holidayhouse.com/I-Like-to-Read/ for more about I Like to Read® books, including flash cards, reproducibles and the complete list of titles.